Let's Take Care of Our New Hamster

Berta García Sabatés and Mercè Segarra / Rosa M. Curto

BARRON'S

Let's adopt a hamster

This is Hairy, a little hamster full of mischief and curiosity, with glossy hair, bright eyes, and furry ears. He looks like a ball of fluff!

And this is the family who has just adopted him. The father, the mother, Mark, and the twins Martha and Mary. Hairy is almost a month old, so he does not need to drink milk from his mother anymore, but as he is still a baby, they will have to handle him very carefully.

Choosing a home

Hairy's new family had never had a hamster at home before, so they are a little lost looking for an adequate cage for him. There are cages in many different shapes. The pet shop clerks said hamsters move around a lot, so the cage for Hairy must have ample room. A twin room cage will be just perfect!

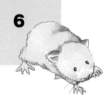

Its own things

Mark has a friend who owns a hamster; that's why he knows Hairy needs to exercise a lot. A wheel for running will be perfect, as well as a horizontal and vertical tube tunnel, so he can enjoy running through them. Mom says hamsters also enjoy boxes with multiple openings through which they can crawl. Finally, after all these considerations, the twins choose a home for Hairy to live in. It is orange and yellow, which are the colors of the desert, where most of the hamsters come from!

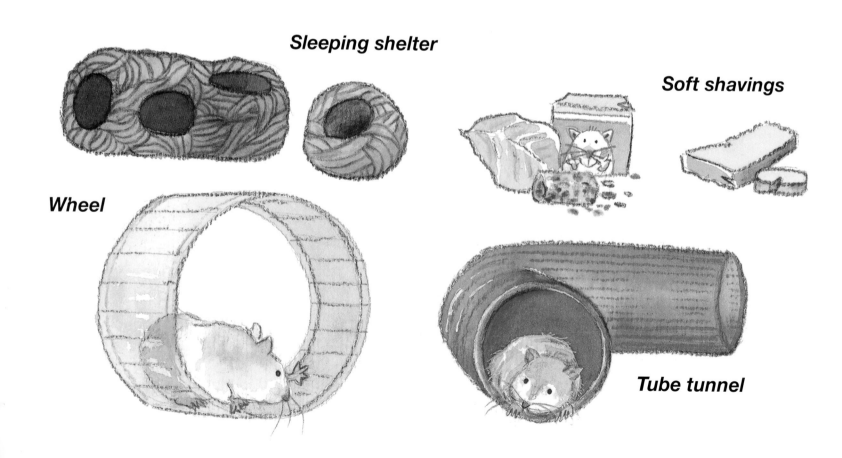

Sleeping shelter

Soft shavings

Wheel

Tube tunnel

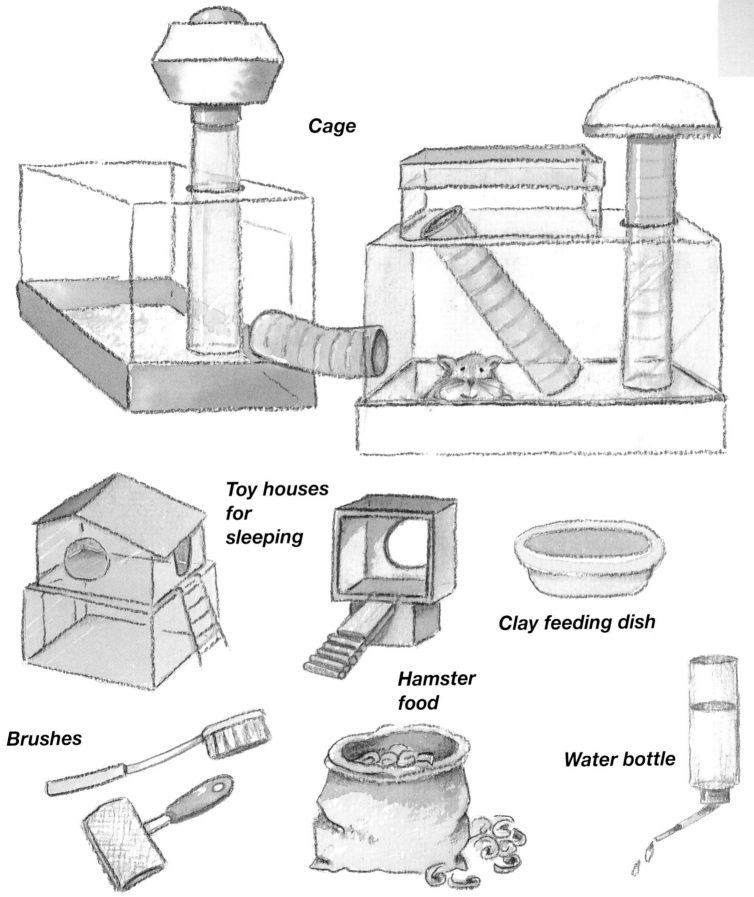

Cage

Toy houses for sleeping

Clay feeding dish

Hamster food

Brushes

Water bottle

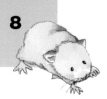

Very careful now!

When they arrived home, Dad said, "We should not disturb Hairy this first day with us, to allow him time to settle in."

Anyway, we don't have to let Hairy
feel lonely any longer than a day,
because he is just a baby, and he will
have to be handled frequently from
now on. This way he will remain docile
and will rarely bite. The sooner Hairy is
handled, the more easily he will begin
to trust us.

They started feeding him some tasty treats such as a slice of apple, a little piece of carrot, and a floret of cauliflower . . . Before taking anything, Hairy sniffs the food, and when he sees that it's good, he carries it away in his cheek pouches

First feeding

and stores it in his burrow. Mark said to the twins, "Never put your fingers inside the cage! He can bite you!"

A busy night

Hairy, like all hamsters, usually sleeps during the day and wakes up in the evening. That is a problem, because when everybody is asleep, then you can hear *nyic, nyic, nyic . . .* Guess what it is? It's Hairy exercising in his wheel! Better close the door or nobody will get any sleep.

Everything in order

Mark also knows that he has to clean out Hairy's bathroom space every day. Hamsters like to amass treasure chests of tidbits, so Mark has to check for stockpiles of perishable food. He also has to change all the bedding twice a week, disinfecting the cage and letting it dry before laying down fresh bedding and replacing the hamster's chewing, nesting, and climbing toys.

Martha and Mary like to give Hairy some paper towels so he can make his own bed. He tears the paper in small pieces, puts them all together and makes a very comfortable bed.

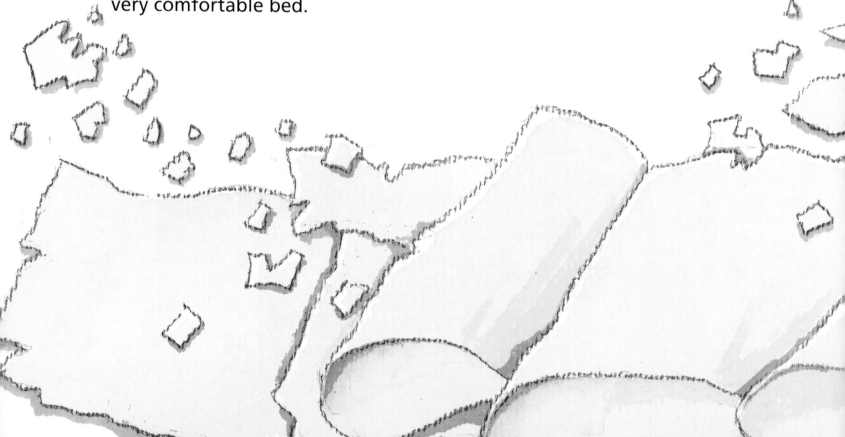

A little work

The best time to feed hamsters is in the evening, so the food doesn't dry out during the day. The pet shop clerk said they would have to clean the water bottle and sipper tube daily to prevent a buildup of food and check that it is working properly. He also said it was very important to fill the water bottle with fresh water every day.

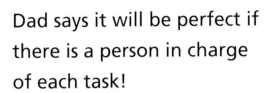

Dad says it will be perfect if there is a person in charge of each task!

Nice and clean

Hairy is so clean that the first thing he does when he wakes up is wash his face and whiskers. He passes his tiny paws over them many times until he is nice and clean. And then . . . time for breakfast!

Mom jokes saying that maybe they should say supper, because when Hairy gets up, the sun is starting to go down.

A handy cup

Hairy, like most hamsters, is a solitary animal. But that does not mean he does not like playing with the children in the family, now that he knows them. When it's time to carry Hairy, Mark, who is already twelve years old, holds his hands together forming a cup. This way they can carry Hairy from one place to another without dropping him.

Mary and Martha will have to wait until they are a little older before they are allowed to carry him!

Special pockets

"Hairy is a glutton!" says Mark. Hairy has put so much food in his mouth that his face looks like a ball. Mark's father tells him that is Hairy's way to carry food from one place to another. It is as if he had some special pockets in his cheeks. When he wants to empty his face pouches, he rubs his cheeks with his paws. Can you imagine if we could do the same?

Sharpening teeth

Hamsters are rodents, which means they chew hard things such as wood or dry bread and if you are not careful, any other object you leave close to their cage. Their teeth keep growing all the time, so if they did not bite and chew, they would become too long. That's why there is always a fresh supply of sticks in Hairy's cage!

A bite

Saturday morning Mary wanted to play with Hairy whether he liked it or not. She is a little impatient and as Hairy was asleep, she started shaking his cage and poking her finger to wake him up. Hairy was so startled that he bit her finger. Mary made a big fuss!

Hamster feelings

The twins can already tell when their hamster feels like playing and when he does not. If they are quiet and relaxed, Hairy will sense that the atmosphere is calm. Hamsters don't like stress!

The twins should never push Hairy into an activity that he resists. Any force could be stressful for him. Hamsters don't like to be moved abruptly, as this can cause them to fear for their lives!

Taking a walk

Now that Hairy and his family have become friends, he may leave his cage for a while and take a walk or run around in the bathtub. If they let him loose on the floor, he could get lost and someone might inadvertently step on him. There are many dangers in a home for such a small pet!

Getting into holes may be harmful.

Some plants are poisonous for him.

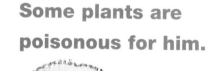

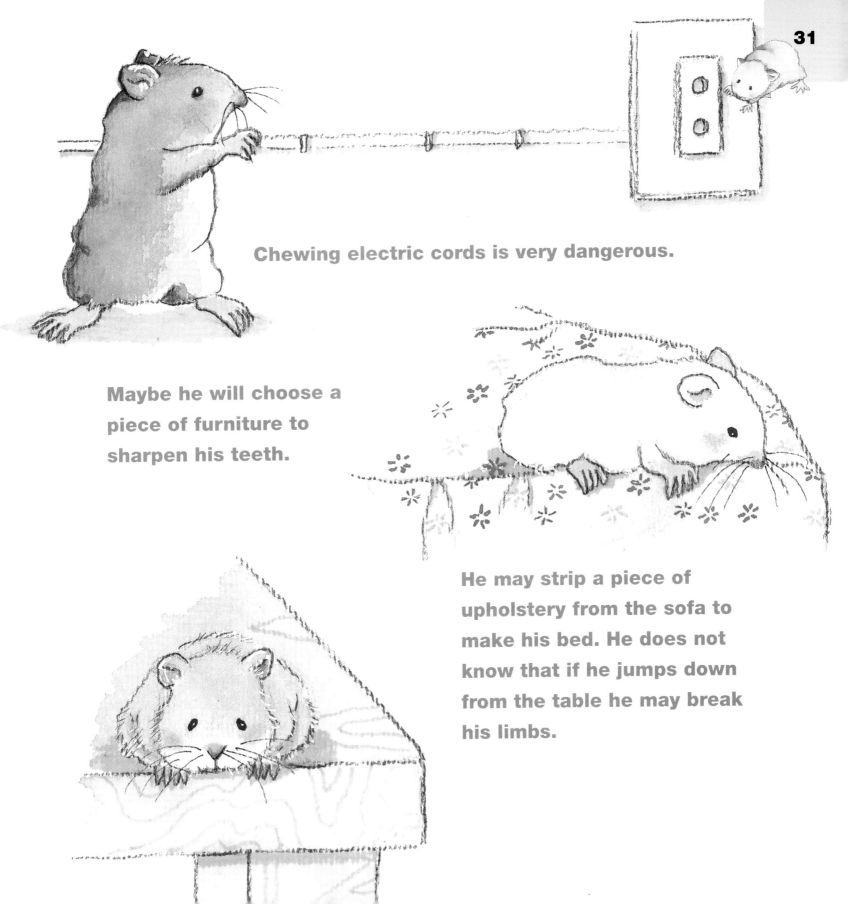

Chewing electric cords is very dangerous.

Maybe he will choose a piece of furniture to sharpen his teeth.

He may strip a piece of upholstery from the sofa to make his bed. He does not know that if he jumps down from the table he may break his limbs.

Hamster food

Hamsters eat a little of everything: seeds, cereals, vegetables, fruit ... Mark knows this does not mean they may feed him just anything. They should not give him any kind of grass or dried fruits because they could be very bad for him. In addition to a grain mixture, hamsters need fresh fruit or vegetables every day, as well as a small amount of animal protein in the form of mealworms, cottage cheese, or yogurt. Taking care of a hamster is a great responsibility as well as a source of surprises, because each hamster has its own personality. Finding it out has been a lot of fun!

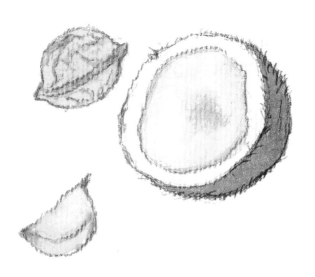

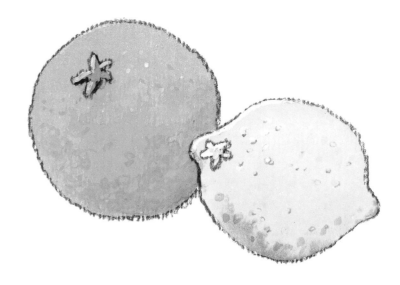

MAGNET

You can make this practical hamster magnet to use on the refrigerator. It can hold the list of foods you will have to buy for your own hamster.

Material: red clay, button-size magnet, clay varnish, card stock, pencil, scissors, awl, scraper, and glue.

Directions:

1. On the card stock, trace the template of the hamster in the illustration and then cut it out.
2. Knead a piece of clay and make a layer about 3/4 inch (2 cm) thick at the most.
3. Mark the silhouette of the hamster on the layer of clay.
4. Use the scraper to shape the hamster out of the piece of clay.
5. With the awl, mark the eye and draw the lines in the hamster for the ears, legs, and mouth. Let the piece dry.
6. When it is dry, apply some varnish to it and let it dry again.
7. Finally, glue the magnet to the back of the clay hamster and let dry.

Activity

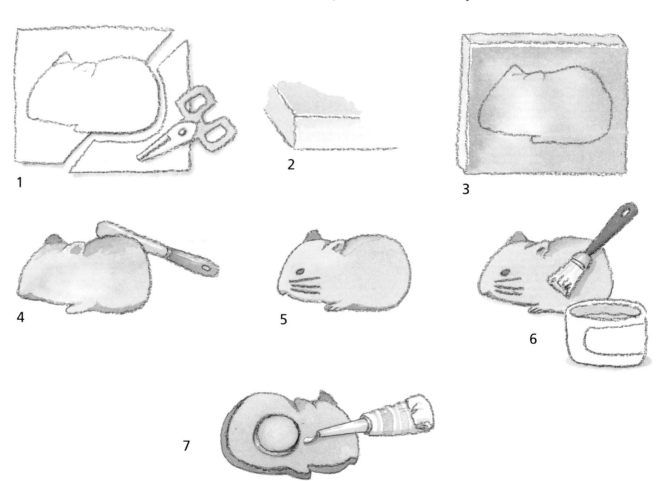

Guidelines from the veterinarian

How to pick up and carry a hamster

If you are not yet twelve years old, you'd better not pick up your hamster. Let a grownup do it. There are two acceptable methods for picking up a hamster. You may use whichever is easier for you. **CAUTION:** Always handle hamsters over a bench or table, because they are liable to jump from your grasp and injure themselves. Either cup your hands and place them over the hamster. Gently press your palms against the animal as you pick it up.

Or, grasp the loose fold of skin behind the neck with your thumb and index finger. Cup your other hand under the animal's rump and grasp the hind legs between your thumb and index finger. Carry the hamster in the same position in which you picked it up.

Buying one or two hamsters?

Golden hamsters are solitary animals. That means that when they grow up, they look for their own territory, which they mark by their scent, and dig their own den. One of the things they don't like is other hamsters, so they have to be kept separate. If you put two hamsters in a regular cage, they are likely to fight and bite each other. However, Russian and Chinese hamsters will live happily in groups if they grow up together.

Food

When they are three weeks old, they stop sucking and start eating a little of everything, because they are omnivorous. They like seeds, fruits, vegetables, and insects. The best for them is to buy a special food mix and add some fresh vegetables and fruit, but just a little bit of everything. The best feeding time is around sunset. Next morning, take away the food left over so it will not go bad.

Teeth

Hamsters are rodents, which means they are always chewing something hard, such as wood or dry bread. This helps them sharpen their teeth and also prevents their teeth from growing too long, because a hamster's teeth keep growing for a lifetime without stopping. If they didn't sharpen their teeth, they would grow so long it would be very uncomfortable for the hamsters. They would even have a hard time eating.

Don't wake your hamster up!

Hamsters are active at night and sleep during the day in their bed, rolling themselves into a ball and hiding their head under their belly. Even though your hamster may be a domestic animal, it may get scared if you wake it up all of a sudden, and it can bite you. You must leave it alone while it is sleeping. If you respect your pet, it will eventually learn to trust you.

Cages

Hamsters are very clean animals and they like to have a place to sleep, a toilet space and some place to keep food in case they feel hungry. That's why the cage for your hamster must be big enough so your pet can arrange this distribution. And remember, your hamster is a rodent, which means its cage must be made of a material that can bear its teeth. The bars in the cage must be horizontal, that way your pet will be able to climb the walls. The best cages are two stories and connected by ramps for a good distribution of the space. There are plastic cages that imitate their natural dens. They have different rooms connected by tunnels. They are perfect.

Bedding

There are many kinds of litter material for the cage. The clerks at the pet store will advise you which one will be best for your hamster. Make sure the litter material will not dirty its hair, can absorb all wetness, and is always clean. Your hamster needs a good litter material in its cage to stay in good condition.

Dangers at home

Your pet may only be allowed out of its cage when it accepts being held in your hands. Hamsters love holes and narrow cracks, so you cannot let your pet free in a room. Remember that sometimes hamsters may go in some small space but then it might be impossible to make them come out again. If they climb somewhere, they just drop as if they don't realize how high that place is, whether it is a table or your hand. Be careful, then, and don't let your hamster climb some place high because it may break its limbs if it jumps down, even if the place is not too high. Other problems: chewing phone or electric wires, tearing away wallpaper or upholstery to make it into some material for its den, eating plants . . . As you can see, you will have to keep a close eye on your pet!

Exercise

Your hamster needs to exercise to keep healthy; that's why the cage should be big enough and have a wheel so it can run inside it. Tube tunnels are also a favorite for a hamster. You might let your pet try a sort of transparent ball, that it can get inside and make it roll around the house. But you must never leave your pet alone inside the rolling ball. It may use it just for a short time every day, always with a grownup watching over it.

LET'S TAKE CARE OF OUR NEW HAMSTER

First edition for the United States and
Canada published in 2008 by
Barron's Educational Series, Inc.

Original title of the book in Catalan: *Un Hámster en Casa*
© Copyright GEMSER PUBLICATIONS, S.L., 2007
C/ Castell, 38 Teià (08329) Barcelona, Spain (World Rights)
Tel: 93 540 13 53
E-mail: info@mercedesros.com
Authors: Berta García Sabatés and Mercè Segarra
Illustrator: Rosa María Curto

All inquiries should be addressed to:
Barron's Educational Series, Inc.
250 Wireless Blvd.
Hauppauge, NY 11788
www.barronseduc.com

ISBN-10: 0-7641-3872-3
ISBN-13: 978-0-7641-3872-0

Library of Congress Control No.: 2007936501

Printed in China
9 8 7 6 5 4 3 2 1